**by ANNETTE TISON and TALUS TAYLOR**

# BARBAPAPA

Published by Xerox Education Publications, Middletown, Connecticut 06457
By arrangement with
FFP Licensing North America, Inc.
A weekly Reader Book Club Edition

XEROX® is a trademark of Xerox Corporation

Printed in Belgium

Barbapapa was born in a garden.

That day François was watering the flowers.

He was surprised
to see Barbapapa,
but they
became friends
at once.

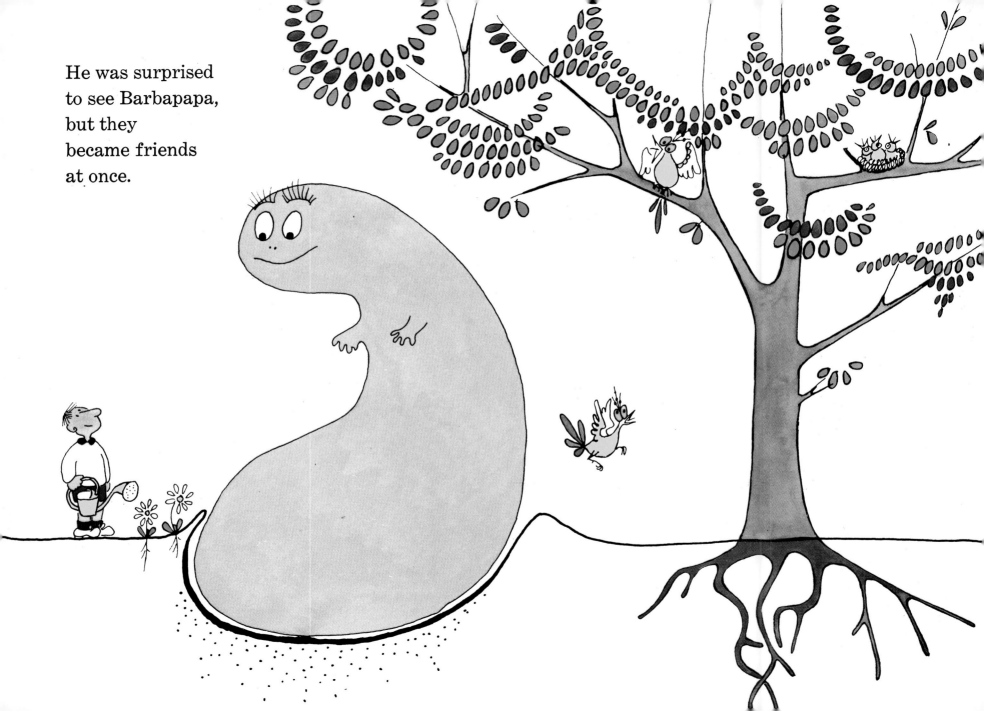

François' mother said that Barbapapa was too big to stay with them.

Barbapapa had to go to the zoo.

He was unhappy because he had to live in a cage.

Barbapapa found he could change his shape and so he escaped.

He wanted to play with the other animals.

He tried to make friends,

but they didn't understand.

The director of the zoo was very angry because Barbapapa had left his cage,

and he ordered Barbapapa to leave the zoo for ever.

Barbapapa wandered into the city but the cars frightened him.

There was nowhere he could go.

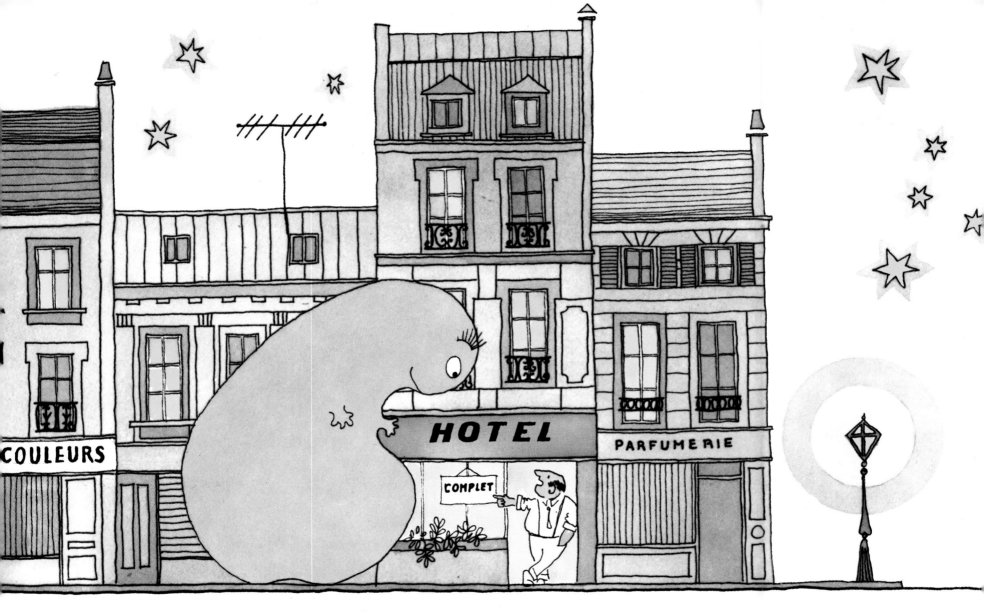

He had no money and no friends.

Barbapapa was all alone and he cried.

But look! A fire!

Barbapapa came to the rescue.

The firemen were grateful for his help.

While they were having a party after the fire, Barbapapa heard cries for help.

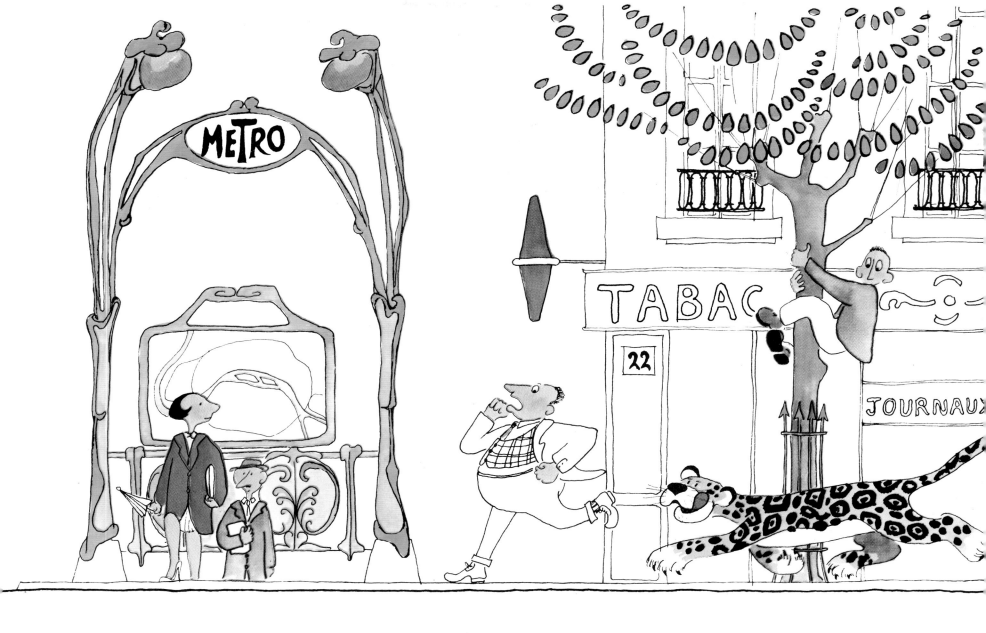

A fierce leopard had escaped from the zoo.

Barbapapa caught him quite easily.

The leopard was returned to the zoo in time for dinner.

Barbapapa became famous.

The city gave him a hero's welcome.

Barbapapa came back to live with François.

François' parents were delighted.

François' father built a house for Barbapapa.

Barbapapa played with the children.

Sometimes Barbapapa met his friends in the park,

and everyone was happy to see him.

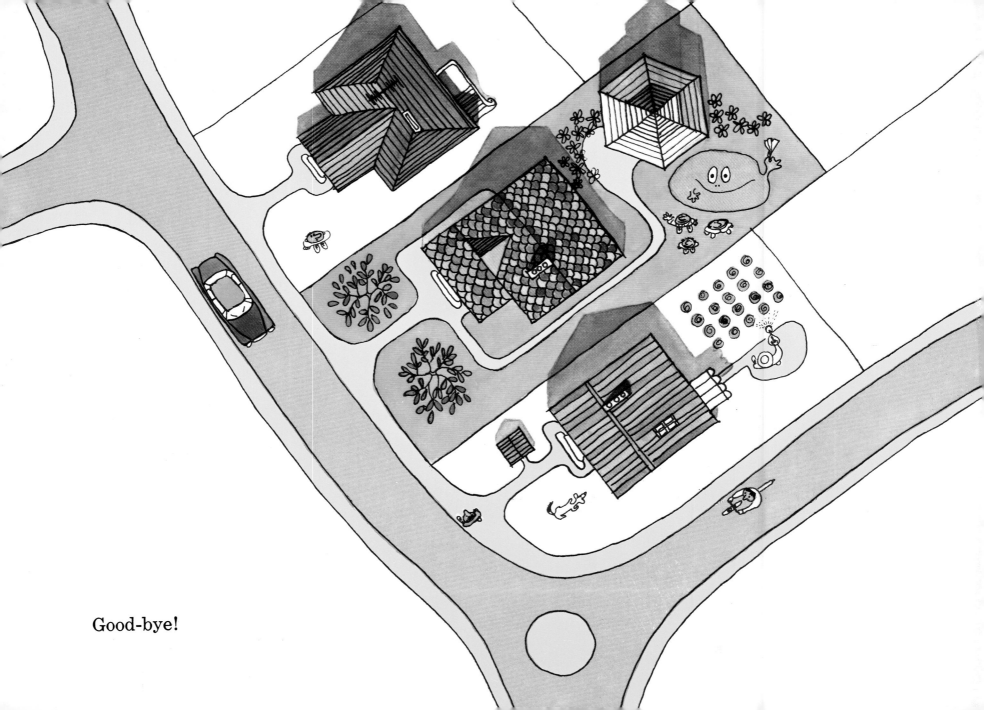

Good-bye!